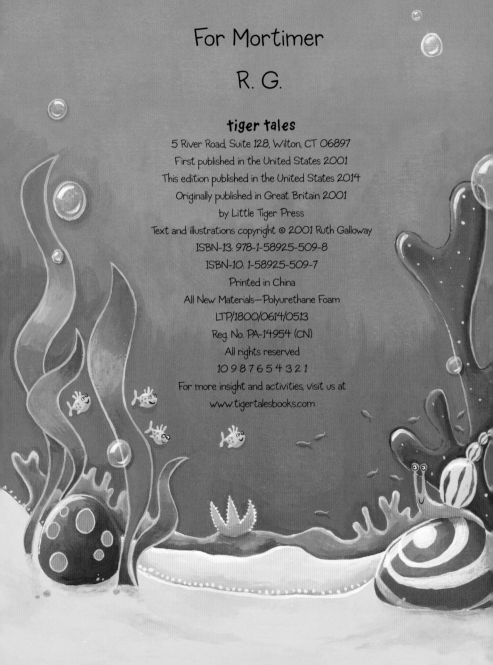

For Mortimer

R. G.

tiger tales

5 River Road, Suite 128, Wilton, CT 06897

First published in the United States 2001

This edition published in the United States 2014

Originally published in Great Britain 2001

by Little Tiger Press

Text and illustrations copyright © 2001 Ruth Galloway

ISBN-13: 978-1-58925-509-8

ISBN-10: 1-58925-509-7

Printed in China

All New Materials—Polyurethane Foam

LTP/1800/0614/0513

Reg. No. PA-14954 (CN)

10 9 8 7 6 5 4 3 2 1

For more insight and activities, visit us at

www.tigertalesbooks.com

The Very Fidgety Fish

by Ruth Galloway

tiger  tales

Tiddler was
always fidgeting.

He wriggled
and squiggled,

he darted
and giggled . . .

until his mom got fed up with him.
  "Go out into the sea and
swim until you're tired, but watch
out for the Big Fish," she said.
  So Tiddler swam out of his cave.

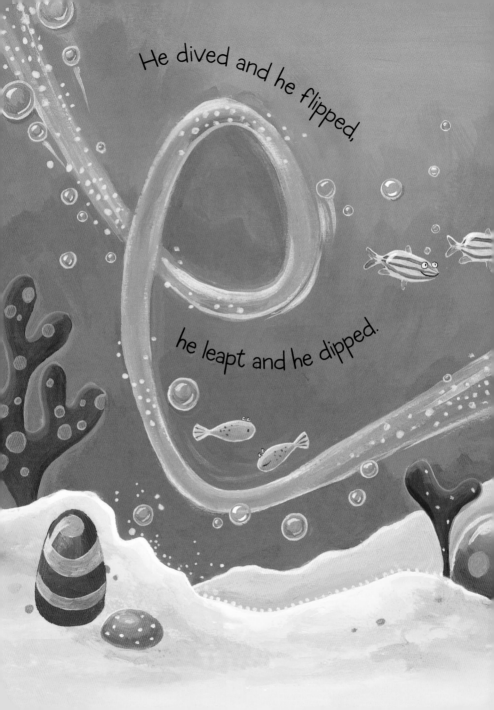

He dived and he flipped,

he leapt and he dipped.

He sped faster than a rocket . . .

and glided gently like a swan,
letting the sea currents fan his fins.

But he still didn't feel tired!

The sea was full of the most interesting things. There were limpets that clung,

and jellyfish that stung.

There was a big, big starfish
that didn't do much at all.

"Hello," said Tiddler, nudging
the starfish gently with his nose.
The starfish didn't answer. It
didn't even move.

A crab sidled by, clicking
and clacking its big claws.
Tiddler wanted to play with it.
But the crab scuttled off and
disappeared into the seaweed.

Tiddler came to a big, dark cave.
It looked much more exciting
than his cave back home,
and Tiddler swam in . . . .

SNAP!

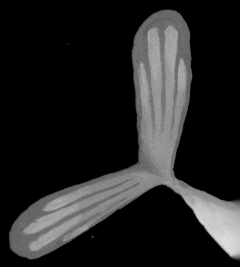

Everything went dark.

Tiddler was trapped inside the Big Fish!

. . . until the Big Fish's tummy
began to feel very funny indeed.
It rumbled and grumbled,
it turned and it tumbled.
It fluttered and groaned,
and mumbled and moaned.

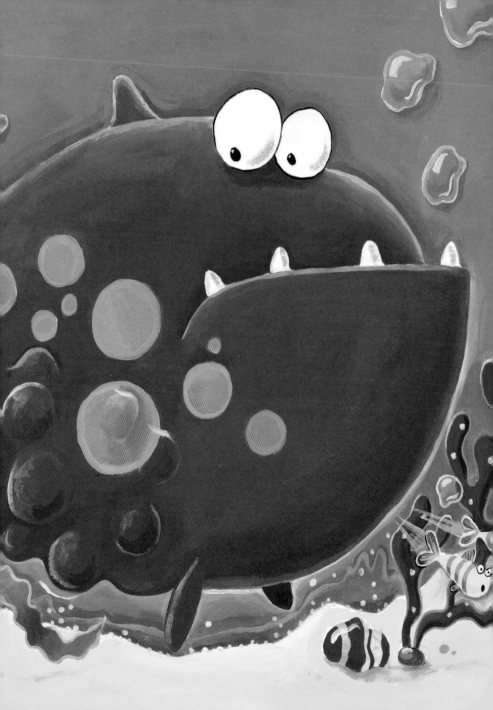

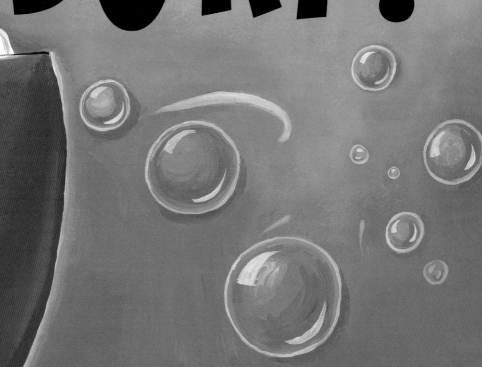

Suddenly, the Big Fish let out a

BURP!

And out shot Tiddler.

He shot past the jellyfish,

and the clickety-clackety
crab hiding in the weeds,

past the starfish . . .

and straight through his own front door!
"I hope you've used up all that energy," said his mom.

But she would have to wait
until the morning to hear
about his adventures,
because Tiddler
was already
fast asleep!